YAF
VAN

Vansant, Wayne.
        Stephen Crane's
    The Red Badge of

	DATE DUE	
1595	4-4-07	
1695	8·11·8	
~~163~~		
60	11/13/09	
MAY 2 8 2015		

STEPHEN CRANE'S

THE RED BADGE OF COURAGE

THE GRAPHIC NOVEL

adapted by Wayne Vansant

PUFFIN BOOKS

Visit us at www.abdopub.com

Spotlight, a division of ABDO Publishing Company, is a distributor of high quality reinforced library bound editions for schools and libraries.

This library bound edition is published by arrangement with Penguin Young Readers Group, a member of Penguin Group (USA) Inc.

Library of Congress Cataloging-In-Publication Data

PUFFIN BOOKS
Published by the Penguin Group
Penguin Young Readers Group,
345 Hudson Street, New York, NY 10014 U.S.A.

The Red Badge of Courage Graphic Novel first published by Puffin Books, a division of Penguin Young Readers Group, 2005

A Byron Preiss Book
Byron Preiss Visual Publications
24 West 25th Street, New York, NY 10010

Adapted by Wayne Vansant
Cover art by Don Troiani
Series Editor: Dwight Jon Zimmerman
Series Assistant Editor: April Isaacs
Interior design by M. Postawa and Gilda Hannah
Cover design by M. Postawa

Puffin Books ISBN 0-14-240410-1
ISBN: 1-59961-118-X Reinforced Library Bound Edition

All Spotlight books are reinforced library binding and manufactured in the United States of America.

STEPHEN CRANE'S

THE RED BADGE
OF COURAGE

THE COLD PASSED RELUCTANTLY FROM THE EARTH, AND THE RETIRING FOG REVEALED AN ARMY STRETCHED OUT ON THE HILLS, RESTING.

AS THE LANDSCAPE CHANGED FROM BROWN TO GREEN, THE ARMY AWAKENED, AND BEGAN TO TREMBLE WITH EAGERNESS AT THE NOISE OF RUMORS.

WE'RE GOIN' T' MOVE T'MORRAH SURE...

WE'RE GOIN' WAY UP RIVER, CUT ACROSS, AN' COME AROUND BEHINT 'EM.

TO HIS ATTENTIVE AUDIENCE THE TALL SOLDIER DREW A LOUD AND ELABORATE PLAN OF A VERY BRILLIANT CAMPAIGN. WHEN HE FINISHED, THE BLUE-COATED MEN SCATTERED INTO SMALL ARGUING GROUPS BETWEEN THE ROWS OF SQUAT BROWN HUTS AND TENTS.

A LOUD PRIVATE TOOK THE MATTER AS AN AFFRONT.

IT'S A LIE, THAT'S ALL IT IS A THUNDERIN' LIE. I DON'T BELIEVE THE DERNED OLD ARMY'S EVER GOING TO MOVE.

WE'RE SET. I'VE GOT READY TO MOVE EIGHT TIMES IN THE LAST TWO WEEKS, AND WE AIN'T MOVED YET.

THE TALL SOLDIER FELT CALLED UPON TO DEFEND THE TRUTH OF A RUMOR HE HIMSELF HAD INTRODUCED. HE AND THE LOUD ONE CAME NEAR TO FIGHTING OVER IT.

MANY OF THE MEN ENGAGED IN A SPIRITED DEBATE. ONE OUTLINED IN A PECULIARLY LUCID MANNER ALL THE PLANS OF THE COMMANDING GENERAL.

HE WAS OPPOSED BY MEN WHO ADVOCATED THAT THERE WERE OTHER PLANS OF. CAMPAIGN.

THEY CLAMORED AT EACH OTHER, NUMBERS MAKING FUTILE BIDS FOR THE POPULAR ATTENTION.

THERE WAS A YOUTHFUL PRIVATE WHO LISTENED WITH EAGER EARS TO THE WORDS OF THE TALL SOLDIER AND THE VARIED COMMENTS OF HIS COMRADES.

AFTER RECEIVING A FILL OF DISCUSSIONS CONCERNING MARCHES AND ATTACKS, HE WENT TO HIS HUT.

HE WISHED TO BE ALONE WITH SOME THOUGHTS THAT HAD LATELY COME TO HIM.

HE LAY DOWN ON HIS BUNK. SO THEY WERE AT LAST GOING TO FIGHT. ON THE MORROW, PERHAPS, THEY WOULD BE A BATTLE, AND HE WOULD BE IN IT. HE COULD NOT ACCEPT WITH ASSURANCE AN OMEN THAT HE WAS ABOUT TO MINGLE IN ONE OF THOSE GREAT AFFAIRS OF THE EARTH.

HE HAD, OF COURSE, DREAMED OF BATTLES ALL HIS LIFE OF VAGUE AND BLOODY CONFLICTS THAT HAD THRILLED HIM WITH THEIR SWEEP AND FIRE... HE HAD REGARDED BATTLES AS CRIMSON BLOTCHES ON THE PAGES OF THE PAST. HE HAD PUT THEM AS THINGS OF THE BYGONE WITH HIS THOUGHT-IMAGES OF HEAVY CROWNS AND HIGH CASTLES.

FROM HIS HOME HIS YOUTHFUL EYES HAD LOOKED UPON THE WAR IN HIS OWN COUNTRY WITH DISTRUST. IT MUST BE SOME SORT OF PLAY AFFAIR, HE THOUGHT. HE HAD LONG DESPAIRED OF WITNESSING A GREEKLIKE STRUGGLE IN HIS OWN TIME... MEN WERE BETTER NOW, OR, AT LEAST MORE TIMID.

HE HAD BURNED SEVERAL TIMES TO ENLIST. TALES OF GREAT MOVEMENT SHOOK THE LAND. THEY MIGHT NOT BE DISTINCTLY HOMERIC, BUT THERE SEEMED TO BE GREAT GLORY IN THEM.

DEFEND THE UNION
A NEW COMPANY IS FORMING OF T
304th NEW YORK
REGIMENT
JOIN TODAY!

BUT HIS MOTHER HAD DISCOURAGED HIM.

MA, I'M GOING TO ENLIST.

HENRY, DON'T YOU BE A FOOL.

NEVERTHELESS, THE NEXT MORNING HE HAD GONE TO A TOWN THAT WAS NEAR HIS MOTHER'S FARM AND ENLISTED IN A COMPANY THAT WAS FORMING THERE.

WHEN HE HAD RETURNED HOME HIS MOTHER WAS MILKING THE BRINDLE COW.

MA, I'VE ENLISTED.

THE LORD'S WILL BE DONE, HENRY.

WHEN HE HAD STOOD IN THE DOORWAY WITH HIS SOLDIER'S CLOTHES ON HIS BACK, HE HAD SEEN TWO TEARS LEAVING THEIR TRAILS ON HIS MOTHER'S SCARRED CHEEKS.

SHE HAD DISAPPOINTED HIM BY SAYING NOTHING WHATEVER ABOUT RETURNING WITH HIS SHIELD OR ON IT.

SHE THEN CONTINUED TO MILK THE BRINDLE COW.

HE HAD PREPARED CERTAIN SENTENCES WHICH HE THOUGHT COULD BE USED WITH TOUCHING EFFECT. BUT HER WORDS DESTROYED HIS PLANS.

YOU WATCH OUT, HENRY, AND TAKE GOOD CARE OF YOURSELF IN THIS FIGHTING BUSINESS. DON'T GO ATHINKIN' YOU CAN LICK THE HULL REBEL ARMY AT THE START, BECAUSE YEH CAN'T.

I'VE KNET YEH EIGHT PAIR OF SOCKS, HENRY, AND I'VE PUT IN ALL YER BEST SHIRTS, BECAUSE I WANT MY BOY TO BE JEST AS WARM AND COMFORTABLE AS ANYBODY IN THE ARMY.

AN' ALLUS BE CAREFUL AN CHOOSE YER COMPANY. THERE'S A LOT OF BAD MEN IN THE ARMY, HENRY. THE ARMY MAKES THEM WILD.

I DON'T WANT YEH TO EVER DO ANYTHING, HENRY, THAT YEH WOULD BE ASHAMED TO LET ME KNOW ABOUT.

10

YEH MUST ALLUS REMEMBER YER FATHER, TOO, CHILD, AN' REMEMBER HE NEVER DRUNK A DROP OF LICKER IN HIS LIFE, AND SELDOM SWORE A CROSS OATH.

I DON'T KNOW WHAT ELSE TO TELL YEH, HENRY, EXCEPTING THAT YEH MUST NEVER DO NO SHIRKING, CHILD, ON MY ACCOUNT. IF SO BE A TIME COMES WHEN YEH HAVE TO BE KILT OR DO A MEAN THING, WHY, HENRY, DON'T THINK OF ANYTHING EXCEPT WHAT'S RIGHT...

...BECAUSE THERE'S MANY A WOMAN HAS TO BEAR UP AGAINST SECH THINGS THESE TIMES, AND THE LORD WILL TAKE CARE OF US ALL.

WHEN HE LOOKED BACK FROM THE GATE, HE HAD SEEN HIS MOTHER KNEELING AMONG THE POTATO PARINGS. HER BROWN FACE, UPRAISED, WAS STAINED WITH TEARS, AND HER SPARE FORM WAS QUIVERING

HE BOWED HIS HEAD AND WENT ON, FEELING SUDDENLY ASHAMED OF HIS PURPOSE.

11

FROM HIS HOME HE HAD GONE TO THE SEMINARY TO BID ADIEU TO MANY SCHOOLMATES. THEY HAD THRONGED ABOUT HIM WITH WONDER AND ADMIRATION. HE FELT THE GULF NOW BETWEEN THEM AND HAD SWELLED WITH CALM PRIDE.

HE AND SOME OF HIS FELLOWS WHO HAD DONNED BLUE WERE QUITE OVERWHELMED WITH PRIVILEGES FOR ALL OF ONE AFTERNOON, AND IT HAD BEEN A VERY DELICIOUS THING...THEY HAD STRUTTED.

A CERTAIN LIGHT-HAIRED GIRL HAD MADE VIVACIOUS FUN AT HIS MARTIAL SPIRIT...

...BUT THERE WAS ANOTHER AND DARKER GIRL WHOM HE HAD GAZED AT STEADFASTLY, AND HE THOUGHT SHE GREW DEMURE AND SAD AT THE SIGHT OF HIS BLUE AND BRASS.

ON THE WAY TO WASHINGTON HIS SPIRIT HAD SOARED. THE REGIMENT WAS FED AND CARESED AT STATION AFTER STATION UNTIL THE YOUTH HAD BELIEVED THAT HE MUST BE A HERO.

AFTER COMPLICATED JOURNEYING WITH MANY PAUSES, THERE HAD COME MONTHS OF MONOTONOUS LIFE IN A CAMP. HE HAD HAD THE BELIEF THAT REAL WAR WAS A SERIES OF DEATH STRUGGLES WITH SMALL TIME IN BETWEEN FOR SLEEP AND MEALS;

BUT SINCE HIS REGIMENT HAD COME TO THE FIELD THE ARMY HAD DONE LITTLE BUT SIT STILL AND TRY TO KEEP WARM.

13

14

HE PERCEIVED NOW THAT IT DID NOT GREATLY MATTER WHAT KIND OF SOLDIER HE WAS GOING TO FIGHT, SO LONG AS THEY FOUGHT, WHICH FACT NO ONE DISPUTED.

THERE WAS A MORE SERIOUS PROBLEM. HE LAY IN HIS BUNK PONDERING UPON IT. HE TRIED TO MATHEMATICALLY PROVE TO HIMSELF THAT HE WOULD NOT RUN FROM A BATTLE.

A LITTLE PANIC-FEAR GREW IN HIS MIND. AS HIS IMAGINATION WENT FORWARD TO A FIGHT, HE SAW HIDEOUS POSSIBILITIES.

THAT'S ALL RIGHT! YOU CAN BELIEVE ME OR NOT, JEST AS YOU LIKE.

PRETTY SOON YOU'LL FIND OUT I WAS RIGHT.

WELL, YOU DON'T KNOW EVERYTHING IN THE WORLD, DO YOU?

16

EARLY ONE MORNING HE FOUND HIMSELF IN THE RANKS OF HIS PREPARED REGIMENT. THE MEN WERE WHISPERING SPECULATIONS AND RECOUNTING THE OLD RUMORS. IN THE GLOOM BEFORE THE BREAK OF DAY, THEIR UNIFORMS GLOWED A DEEP PURPLE HUE.

A MOMENT LATER THE REGIMENT WENT SWINGING OFF INTO THE DARKNESS. IT WAS NOW LIKE ONE OF THOSE MOVING MONSTERS WENDING WITH MANY FEET. THE AIR WAS HEAVY, AND COLD WITH DEW. A MASS OF WET GRASS, MARCHED UPON, RUSTLED LIKE SILK.

THE LONG SERPENTS CRAWLED SLOWLY FROM HILL TO HILL WITHOUT BLUSTER OF SMOKE. A DUNG-COLORED CLOUD OF DUST FLOATED AWAY TO THE RIGHT. THE SKY OVERHEAD WAS A FAIRY BLUE.

19

THE MEN BEGAN TO SPEAK OF VICTORY AS OF A THING THEY KNEW. ALSO. THE TALL SOLDIER RECEIVED HIS VINDICATION.

THE YOUTH, CONSIDERING HIMSELF AS SEPARATED FROM THE OTHERS, WAS SADDENED BY THE BLITHE AND MERRY SPEECHES THAT WENT FROM RANK TO RANK.

A RATHER FAT SOLDIER ATTEMPTED TO PILFER A HORSE FROM A DOORYARD, PLANNING TO LOAD HIS KNAPSACK UPON IT.

HE WAS ESCAPING WITH HIS PRIZE WHEN A YOUNG GIRL RUSHED FROM THE HOUSE AND GRABBED THE ANIMAL'S MANE.

THERE FOLLOWED A WRANGLE. THE YOUNG GIRL, WITH PINK CHEEKS AND SHINING EYES, STOOD LIKE A DAUNTLESS STATUE.

THE OBSERVANT REGIMENT, STANDING AT REST IN THE ROADWAY, WHOOPED AT ONCE, AND ENTERED WHOLE-SOULED UPON THE SIDE OF THE MAIDEN

HIT HIM WITH A STICK!

WHEN HE RETREATED WITHOUT THE HORSE, THE REGIMENT REJOICED.

21

AT NIGHTFALL THE COLUMN BROKE INTO REGIMENTAL PIECES, AND THE FRAGMENTS WENT INTO THE FIELDS TO CAMP.

THE YOUTH KEPT FROM INTERCOURSE WITH HIS COMPANIONS AS MUCH AS CIRCUMSTANCES WOULD ALLOW HIM. IN THE EVENING HE WANDERED A FEW PACES INTO THE GLOOM.

HE WISHED, WITHOUT RESERVE, THAT HE WAS AT HOME AGAIN MAKING THE ENDLESS ROUNDS FROM THE HOUSE TO THE BARN, FROM THE BARN TO THE FIELD, FROM THE FIELD TO THE BARN, FROM THE BARN TO THE HOUSE.

HE REMEMBERED HE HAD OFTEN CURSED THE BRINDLE COW AND HER MATES, BUT, FROM HIS PRESENT POINT OF VIEW, THERE WAS A HALO OF HAPPINESS ABOUT EACH OF THEIR HEADS.

23

24

THE NEXT MORNING THEY CROSSED A PONTOON BRIDGE. THE MEN HAD BEGUN TO COUNT THE MILES UPON THEIR FINGERS, AND THEY GREW TIRED. THEY EXTRICATED THEMSELVES FROM THICK SHIRTS, KEEPING ONLY THEIR NECESSARY CLOTHING, BLANKETS, HAVERSACK, CANTEENS, ARMS AND AMMUNITION.

SORE FEET AN' DAMNED SHORT RATIONS, THAT'S ALL.

YOU CAN NOW EAT AND SHOOT...

...THAT'S ALL YOU WANT TO DO.

THEY WERE NOW AMONG OTHER REGIMENTS AND BRIGADES, AND MANY SHOWED THEIR VETERAN STATUS BY THEIR VARIETY OF HATS AND LETTERS OF FADED GOLD SPEAKING FROM THEIR COLORS.

SOUTH M...
FREDERICKSBUR...

THE SOUNDS OF BATTLE COULD BE HEARD IN THE NEAR DISTANCE.

25

SUDDENLY THE ENTIRE REGIMENT FOUND THEMSELVES RUNNING DOWN A WOOD ROAD, THE MEN PANTING FROM THE FIRST EFFECTS OF SPEED. THE SUN SPREAD DISCLOSING RAYS, AND, ONE BY ONE, REGIMENTS BURST INTO VIEW LIKE ARMED MEN JUST BORN OF THE EARTH

SAY... WHAT'S ALL THIS... ABOUT?

WHAT TH' THUNDER WE SKEDADDLIN' THIS WAY FER?

THE YOUTH PERCEIVED THAT THE TIME HAD COME.

HE INSTANTLY SAW THAT IT WOULD BE IMPOSSIBLE FOR HIM TO ESCAPE FROM THE REGIMENT. IT INCLOSED HIM.

THE REGIMENT SLID DOWN A BANK AND WALLOWED ACROSS A LITTLE STREAM. AS THEY CLIMBED THE HILL ON THE FARTHER SIDE ARTILLERY BEGAN TO BOOM.

THERE WERE SOME LITTLE FIELDS GIRTED AND SQUEEZED BY A FOREST. SPREAD OVER THE GRASS AND IN AMONG THE TREE TRUNKS, HE COULD SEE KNOTS AND WAVING LINES OF SKIRMISHERS WHO WERE RUNNING HITHER AND THITHER AND FIRING AT THE LANDSCAPE. A DARK BATTLE LINE LAY UPON A SUNSTRUCK CLEARING THAT GLEAMED ORANGE COLOR. A FLAG FLUTTERED.

THE LINE ENCOUNTERED THE BODY OF A DEAD SOLDIER. HE LAY UPON HIS BACK STARING AT THE SKY .HE WAS DRESSED IN AN AWKWARD SUIT OF YELLOWISH BROWN.

THE YOUTH COULD SEE THAT THE SOLES OF HIS SHOES HAD BEEN WORN TO THE THINNESS OF WRITING PAPER. IT WAS AS IF FATE HAD BETRAYED THE SOLDIER,

IN DEATH IT EXPOSED TO HIS ENEMIES THAT POVERTY WHICH IN LIFE HE HAD PERHAPS CONCEALED FROM HIS FRIENDS.

ABSURD IDEAS TOOK HOLD UPON THE YOUTH. A HOUSE STANDING IN THE DISTANT FIELD HAD AN OMINOUS LOOK. THE SHADOWS OF THE WOODS WERE FORMIDABLE. HE WAS CERTAIN THAT IN THIS VISTA LURKED FIERCE EYED HOST.

THE SWIFT THOUGHT CAME TO HIM THAT THE GENERALS DID NOT KNOW WHAT THEY WERE ABOUT. IT WAS ALL A TRAP!

HE LOOKED AT THE MEN AROUND HIM, AND SAW, FOR THE MOST PART, EXPRESSIONS OF DEEP INTEREST, AS IF THEY WERE INVESTIGATING SOMETHING THAT HAD FASCINATED THEM. THE GREATER PART OF THE UNTESTED MEN APPEARED QUIET AND ABSORBED.

THEY WERE GOING TO LOOK AT WAR, THE RED ANIMAL WAR, THE BLOOD-SWOLLEN GOD.

29

AFTER A TIME THE BRIGADE WAS HALTED IN THE CATHEDRAL LIGHT OF A FOREST. THE BUSY SKIRMISHERS WERE STILL POPPING. THROUGH THE AISLES OF THE WOODS COULD BE SEEN THE FLOATING SMOKE OF THEIR RIFLES.

DURING THE HALT MANY MEN IN THE REGIMENT BEGAN ERECTING TINY HILLS IN FRONT OF THEM. THEY USED STONES, STICKS, EARTH, AND ANYTHING THEY THOUGHT MIGHT TURN A BULLET.

THIS PROCEDURE CAUSED A DISCUSSION AMONG THE MEN. SOME WISHED TO FIGHT LIKE DUELISTS, BELIEVING IT TO BE CORRECT TO STAND ERECT.

OTHERS SCOFFED IN REPLY, AND POINTED TO THE VETERANS ON THE FLANKS WHO WERE DIGGING AT THE GROUND LIKE TERRIERS.

DIRECTLY, HOWEVER, THEY WERE ORDERED TO WITHDRAW FROM THAT PLACE.

THEY WERE MOVED TO ANOTHER PLACE. THEY ATE THEIR NOON MEAL BEHIND A THIRD ONE. THEY WERE MARCHED FROM PLACE TO PLACE WITH APPARENT AIMLESSNESS.

WELL, THEN WHAT DID THEY MARCH US OUT HERE FOR?

I DON'T SEE WHAT GOOD IT DOES TO WEAR OUT OUR LEGS FOR NOTHIN'.

NEITHER DO I!

IT AIN'T RIGHT! I TELL YOU THAT IF ANYBODY WITH ANY SENSE WAS-A-RUNNING THIS ARMY IT...

THE TALL PRIVATE HAD HEARD ENOUGH...

OH, SHUT UP!

YOU LITTLE FOOL. YOU DAMNED LITTLE CUSS! YOU AIN'T HAD THAT COAT ON FOR SIX MONTHS, AND YET YOU TALK AS IF...

WELL, I WANTA DO SOME FIGHTIN' ANYWAY...

THAT AFTERNOON THE REGIMENT WENT OVER THE SAME GROUND IT HAD TAKEN IN THE MORNING. WHEN THEY BEGAN TO PASS INTO A NEW REGION. HIS OLD FEARS OF STUPIDITY AND INCOMPETENCE REASSAILED HIM.

THE SKIRMISH FIRE INCREASED TO A LONG CHATTERING SOUND. WITH IT WAS MINGLED FAR AWAY CHEERING. A BATTERY SPOKE.

DIRECTLY THE YOUTH WOULD SEE THE SKIRMISHERS RUNNING. THEY WERE PURSUED BY THE SOUND OF MUSKETRY FIRE. AFTER A TIME THE HOT, DANGEROUS FLASHED OF THE RIFLES WERE VISIBLE.

THE DIN BECAME A CRESCENDO, LIKE THE ROAR OF AN ONCOMING TRAIN.

SUDDENLY, THE YOUTH FELT A HEAVY AND SAD HAND LAID ON HIS SHOULDER.

IT'S MY FIRST AND LAST BATTLE, OLD BOY.

EH?

I'M A GONE COON THIS TIME AND AND I W-WANT YOU TO TAKE THESE THINGS TO MY FOLKS.

WHY, WHAT THE DEVIL?

THE LOUD SOLDIER GAVE HIM A GLANCE AS FROM THE DEPTHS OF A TOMB.

THE BRIGADE WAS HALTED IN THE FRINGE OF A GROVE. BULLETS BEGAN TO WHISTLE AMONG THE BRANCHES AND NIP AT THE TREES. TWIGS AND LEAVES CAME SAILING DOWN.

THE LIEUTENANT OF THE YOUTH'S COMPANY WAS SHOT IN THE HAND. HE BEGAN TO SWEAR WONDROUSLY, AS IF HE HAD HIT HIS FINGER WITH A TACK HAMMER AT HOME.

A NERVOUS LAUGHTER WENT ALONG THE REGIMENTAL LINE, RELIEVING THE TIGHTENED SENSES OF THE NEW MEN.

33

THE BATTLE FLAGS IN THE DISTANCE JERKED ABOUT MADLY. THEY SEEMED TO BE STRUGGLING TO FREE THEMSELVES FROM AN AGONY.

MEN RUNNING SWIFTLY EMERGED FROM THE SMOKE. THEY GREW IN NUMBER UNTIL IT WAS SEEN THAT THE WHOLE COMMAND WAS FLEEING

THE VETERAN REGIMENTS ON THE RIGHT AND LEFT BEGAN TO JEER. AT THE FLEEING MEN. WITH THE PASSIONATE SONG OF THE BULLETS AND THE BANSHEE SHRIEKS OF SHELLS WERE MINGLED LOUD CATCALLS AND BITS OF FACETIOUS ADVICE CONCERNING PLACES OF SAFETY.

OVER THIS TUMULT COULD BE HEARD THE GRIM JOKES OF THE CRITICAL VETERANS; BUT THE RETREATING MEN APPARENTLY WERE NOT EVEN CONSCIOUS OF THE PRESENCE OF AN AUDIENCE.

THE COMPOSITE MONSTER WHICH HAD CAUSED THE OTHERS TO FLEE HAD NOT THEN APPEARED. THE YOUTH RESOLVED TO GET A VIEW OF IT, AND THEN, HE THOUGHT HE MIGHT LIKELY RUN BETTER THAN THE BEST OF THEM.

THEN SOMEONE CRIED

HERE THEY COME!

ACROSS THE SMOKE-INFESTED FIELDS CAME A BROWN SWARM OF RUNNING MEN WHO WERE GIVING SHRILL YELLS. THEY CAME ON, STOOPING AND SWINGING THEIR RIFLES AT ALL ANGLES.

A FLAG, TILTED FORWARD, SPED NEAR THE FRONT.

A HATLESS GENERAL PULLED HIS DRIPPING HORSE TO A STAND HEAR THE COLONEL OF THE 304TH.

YOU'VE GOT TO HOLD THEM BACK!

YOU'VE GOT TO HOLD THEM BACK!

A-ALL R-RIGHT, GENERAL, BY GAWD...

WE-WE'LL DO OUR WE-WE'LL D-D-DO OUR BEST, GENERAL.

THE CAPTAIN OF THE COMPANY HAD BEEN PACING EXCITEDLY TO AND FRO. HE COAXED IN SCHOOLMISTRESS FASHION, AS TO A CONGREGATION OF BOYS WITH PRIMERS.

RESERVE YOUR FIRE, BOYS. DON'T SHOOT TILL I TELL YOU.

SAVE YOUR FIRE. WAIT TILL THEY GET CLOSE UP. DON'T BE A DAMNED FOOL.

PERSPIRATION STREAMED DOWN THE YOUTH'S FACE, WHICH WAS SOILED LIKE THAT OF A WEEPING URCHIN. HE FREQUENTLY, WITH A NERVOUS MOVEMENT, WIPED HIS EYES WITH HIS COAT SLEEVE.

HE GOT ONE GLANCE AT THE FOE-SWARMING FIELD IN FRONT OF HIM, AND INSTANTLY CEASED TO DEBATE THE QUESTION OF HIS PIECE BEING LOADED.

39

BEFORE HE WAS READY TO BEGIN, BEFORE HE HAD ANNOUNCED TO HIMSELF THAT HE WAS ABOUT TO FIGHT, HE THREW THE OBEDIENT, WELL-BALANCED RIFLE INTO POSITION AND...

HE SUDDENLY LOST CONCERN FOR HIMSELF, AND FORGOT TO LOOK AT A MENACING FATE. HE BECAME NOT A MAN BUT A MEMBER.

HE FELT THAT SOMETHING OF WHICH HE WAS A PART — A REGIMENT, AN ARMY, A CAUSE, OR A COUNTRY — WAS IN CRISIS. HE WAS WELDED INTO A COMMON PERSONALITY WHICH WAS DOMINATED BY A SINGLE DESIRE.

FOR SOME MOMENTS HE COULD NOT FLEE NO MORE THAN A LITTLE FINGER CAN COMMIT A REVOLUTION FROM A HAND.

THE LIEUTENANT OF THE YOUTH'S COMPANY HAD ENCOUNTERED A SOLDIER WHO HAD FLED SCREAMING AT THE FIRST VOLLEY OF HIS COMRADES.

THE MAN WAS BLUBBERING AND STARING WITH SHEEPLIKE EYES AT THE LIEUTENANT, WHO HAD SEIZED HIM BY THE COLLAR AND WAS POMMELING HIM. HE DROVE HIM BACK INTO THE RANKS WITH MANY BLOWS

THE SOLDIER TRIED TO RELOAD HIS GUN, BUT HIS SHAKING HANDS PREVENTED. THE LIEUTENANT WAS OBLIGED TO ASSIST HIM.

43

THE MEN DROPPED HERE AND
THERE LIKE BUNDLES.

THE CAPTAIN OF THE YOUTH'S COMPANY HAD BEEN KILLED, HIS BODY STRETCHED OUT IN THE POSITION OF A TIRED MAN RESTING.

ANOTHER GRUNTED SUDDENLY AS IF HE HAD BEEN STRUCK BY A CLUB IN THE STOMACH. HE SAT DOWN AND GAZED RUEFULLY.

FARTHER UP THE LINE A MAN, STANDING BEHIND A TREE, HAD HIS KNEE JOINT SPLINTERED BY A BALL. THERE HE REMAINED, CLINGING DESPERATELY TO THE TREE, AND CRYING FOR ASSISTANCE.

AT LAST AN EXULTANT YELL WENT ALONG THE QUIVERING LINE. THE FIRING DWINDLED FROM AN UPROAR TO A LAST VINDICTIVE POPPING.

AS THE SMOKE SLOWLY EDDIED AWAY, THE YOUTH SAW THAT THE CHARGE HAD BEEN REPULSED. THE ENEMY WERE SCATTERED INTO RELUCTANT GROUPS.

SOME OF THE REGIMENT BEGAN TO WHOOP FRENZIEDLY. MANY WERE SILENT. APPARENTLY THEY WERE TRYING TO CONTEMPLATE THEMSELVES.

AFTER THE FEVER HAD LEFT HIS VEINS, THE YOUTH BECAME AWARE OF THE FOUL ATMOSPHERE IN WHICH HE HAD BEEN STRUGGLING.

A SENTENCE WITH VARIATIONS WENT UP AND DOWN THE LINE.

WELL, WE HELT EM BACK. WE HELT EM BACK.

DERNED IF WE HAVEN'T.

HE WAS GRIMY AND DRIPPING LIKE A LABORER IN A FOUNDRY.

THE MEN SAID IT BLISSFULLY, LEERING AT EACH OTHER WITH DIRTY SMILES.

UNDER FOOT WERE A FEW GHASTLY FORMS MOTIONLESS. THEY LAY TWISTED IN FANTASTIC CONTORTIONS.

THEY LOOKED TO BE DUMPED OUT UPON THE GROUND FROM THE SKY.

THE YOUTH AWAKENED SLOWLY. SO IT WAS ALL OVER AT LAST! THE SUPREME TRIAL
HAD BEEN PASSED. THE RED, FORMIDABLE DIFFICULTIES OF WAR HAD BEEN VANQUISHED.

HE HAD THE MOST DELIGHTFUL SENSATIONS
OF HIS LIFE. STANDING AS IF APART FROM
HIMSELF, HE VIEWED THAT LAST SCENE. HE
PERCEIVED THAT THE MAN WHO HAD FOUGHT
THUS WAS MAGNIFICENT.

HE FELT LIKE HE WAS A FINE FELLOW. HE SAW
HIMSELF EVEN WITH THOSE IDEALS WHICH HE
HAD CONSIDERED BEYOND HIM. HE SMILED IN
DEEP GRATIFICATION.

GEE! AIN'T IT HOT, HEY?

YOU BET! I AIN'T NEVER SEEN SECH DUMB HOTNESS.

THERE WAS SOME HANDSHAKES AND DEEP SPEECHES WITH MEN WHOSE FEATURES WERE FAMILIAR, BUT WITH WHOM THE YOUTH NOW FELT THE BONDS OF TIRED HEARTS.

I HOPE WE DON'T HAVE NO MORE FIGHTIN' TILL A WEEK FROM MONDAY.

BUT, OF A SUDDEN, CRIES OF AMAZEMENT BROKE OUT ALONG THE RANKS OF THE NEW REGIMENT.

HERE THEY COME AGAIN!

HERE THEY COME AGAIN!

THE YOUTH TURNED QUICK EYES UPON THE FIELD. HE DISCERNED FORMS BEGIN TO SWELL IN MASSES OUT OF A DISTANT WOOD. HE AGAIN SAW THE TILTED FLAG SPEEDING FORWARD.

THE MEN GROANED. THE LUSTER FADED FROM THEIR EYES. THEIR SMUDGED COUNTENANCES NOW EXPRESSED A PROFOUND DEJECTION.

THE YOUTH STARED. SURELY, HE THOUGHT, THIS IMPOSSIBLE THING WAS NOT ABOUT TO HAPPEN. HE WAITED AS IF HE EXPECTED THE ENEMY TO SUDDENLY STOP, APOLOGIZE, AND RETIRE BOWING. IT WAS ALL A MISTAKE.

OH, SAY, THIS IS TOO MUCH OF A GOOD THING...

...WHY CAN'T SOMEBODY SEND US SUPPORTERS?

TO THE YOUTH IT WAS AN ONSLAUGHT OF REDOUBTABLE DRAGONS. HE BECAME LIKE THE MAN WHO LOST HIS LEGS AT THE APPROACH OF THE RED AND GREEN MONSTER.

A MAN NEAR HIM WHO UP TO THIS TIME HAD BEEN WORKING FEVERISHLY AT HIS RIFLE SUDDENLY STOPPED AND RAN WITH HOWLS.

A LAD WHOSE FACE HAD BORNE AN EXPRESSION OF EXALTED COURAGE, THREW DOWN HIS GUN AND FLED. THERE WAS A REVELATION. THERE WAS NO SHAME ON HIS FACE.

HE RAN LIKE A RABBIT.

OTHERS BEGAN TO SCAMPER AWAY THROUGH THE SMOKE. HE SAW THE FEW FLEETING FORMS.

HE YELLED THEN WITH FRIGHT AND SWUNG ABOUT.

FOR A MOMENT, HE LOST THE DIRECTION OF SAFETY. DESTRUCTION THREATENED HIM FROM ALL POINTS.

DIRECTLY HE BEGAN TO SPEED TOWARD THE REAR IN GREAT LEAPS. HIS RIFLE AND CAP WERE GONE. HIS UNBUTTONED COAT BULGED IN THE WIND. THE FLAP OF HIS CARTRIDGE BOX BOBBED WILDLY, AND HIS CANTEEN, BY ITS SLENDER CORD, SWUNG OUT BEHIND.

HE RAN LIKE A BLIND MAN. TWO OR THREE TIMES HE FELL DOWN. ONCE HE KNOCKED HIS SHOULDER SO HEAVILY AGAINST A TREE THAT HE WENT HEADLONG.

SINCE HE HAD TURNED HIS BACK UPON THE FIGHT HIS FEARS HAD BEEN WONDROUSLY MAGNIFIED. DEATH ABOUT TO THRUST HIM BETWEEN THE SHOULDER BLADES WAS FAR MORE DREADFUL THAN DEATH ABOUT TO SMITE HIM BETWEEN THE EYES.

AS HE RAN HE MINGLED WITH OTHERS. IN HIS FLIGHT THE SOUND OF THESE FOLLOWING FOOTSTEPS GAVE HIM ONE MEAGER RELIEF.

HE EXPERIENCED A THRILL OF AMAZEMENT WHEN HE CAME WITHIN VIEW OF A BATTERY IN ACTION. THE MEN THERE SEEMED TO BE IN CONVENTIONAL MOODS, ALTOGETHER UNAWARE OF THE IMPENDING ANNIHILATION.

THE YOUTH PITIED THEM AS HE RAN. METHODICAL IDIOTS! MACHINE-LIKE FOOLS! THE REFINED JOY OF PLANTING SHELLS IN THE MIDST OF THE OTHER BATTERY'S FORMATION WOULD APPEAR A LITTLE THING WHEN THE INFANTRY CAME SWOOPING OUT OF THE WOODS.

55

THE YOUTH WENT ON, MODERATING HIS PACE SINCE HE HAD LEFT THE PLACE OF NOISES. HE CAME UPON A GENERAL OF DIVISION SEATED UPON A HORSE THAT PRICKED ITS EARS IN AN INTERESTED WAY AT THE BATTLE. HE WENT AS NEAR AS HE DARED TRYING TO OVERHEAR WORDS. OTHER MOUNTED MEN CIRCLED AROUND HIM.

A MOMENT LATER THE YOUTH SAW THE GENERAL BOUNCE EXCITEDLY IN THE SADDLE FROM SOME INFORMATION HE HAD JUST RECEIVED.

THE YOUTH CRINGED AS IF DISCOVERED IN A CRIME. BY HEAVENS, THEY HAD WON AFTER ALL! THE IMBECILE LINE HAD REMAINED AND BECOME VICTORS.

HE COULD HEAR CHEERING.

HE TURNED AWAY AMAZED AND ANGRY. HE FELT THAT HE HAD BEEN WRONGED.

THOUGHTS OF HIS COMRADES CAME TO HIM. THE BRITTLE BLUE LINE HAD WITHSTOOD THE BLOWS AND WON. HE GREW BITTER OVER IT. IT SEEMED THAT THE BLIND IGNORANCE AND STUPIDITY OF THESE LITTLE PIECES HAD BETRAYED HIM.

HE WONDERED WHAT THEY WOULD REMARK WHEN LATER HE APPEARED IN CAMP. HIS MIND HEARD HOWLS OF DERISION. THEIR DENSITY WOULD NOT ENABLE THEM TO UNDERSTAND HIS SHARPER POINT OF VIEW.

HE WENT FROM THE FIELD INTO A THICK WOOD, AS IF RESOLVED TO BURY HIMSELF. HE WISHED TO GET OUT OF THE HEARING OF THE CRACKING SHOTS WHICH WERE TO HIM LIKE VOICES.

THE GROUND WAS CLUTTERED WITH VINES AND BUSHES, AND THE TREES GREW CLOSE AND SPREAD OUT LIKE BOUQUETS. HE WAS OBLIGED TO FORCE HIS WAY WITH MUCH NOISE.

HE THREW A PINE CONE AT A JOVIAL SQUIRREL, AND HE WATCHED IT RUN AWAY WITH CHATTERING.

THE YOUTH FELT TRIUMPHANT AT THIS EXHIBITION. NATURE HAD GIVEN HIM A SIGN...

58

AT LENGTH HE REACHED A PLACE WHERE THE HIGH, ARCHING BOUGHS MADE A CHAPEL. PINE NEEDLES WERE A GENTLE BROWN CARPET. THERE WAS A RELIGIOUS HALF-LIGHT.

NEAR THE THRESHOLD HE STOPPED, HORROR-STRICKEN AT THE SIGHT OF THE THING.

HE WAS BEING LOOKED AT BY A DEAD MAN WHO WAS SEATED WITH HIS BACK AGAINST A TREE. THE CORPSE WAS DRESSED IN A UNIFORM THAT ONCE HAD BEEN BLUE, BUT WAS NOW FADED TO A MELANCHOLY SHADE OF GREEN.

OVER THE GRAY SKIN OF THE FACE RAN LITTLE ANTS,

THE YOUTH GRADUALLY BEGAN TO BACK AWAY FROM THE THING, ALL THE TIME FACING HIM. HE FEARED THAT IF HE TURNED HIS BACK THE BODY MIGHT SPRING UP AND STEALTHILY PURSUE HIM.

WHEN THE TREES BEGAN SOFTLY TO SING A HYMN OF TWILIGHT, THE YOUTH SUDDENLY STOPPED. THERE SUDDENLY BROKE A TREMENDOUS CLANGOR OF SOUNDS.

HE BEGAN TO RUN IN THE DIRECTION OF THE BATTLE. HE SAW THAT IT WAS AN IRONICAL THING FOR HIM TO BE RUNNING THUS TOWARD THAT WHICH HE HAD BEEN AT SUCH PAINS TO AVOID.

PRESENTLY HE WAS WHERE HE COULD SEE LONG GRAY WALLS OF VAPOR WHERE LAY BATTLE LINES. THE VOICES OF CANNON SHOOK HIM. THE MUSKETRY SOUNDED IN LONG IRRUGULAR SURGES THAT PLAYED HAVOC WITH HIS EARS. HE STOOD REGARDANT FOR A MOMENT. HIS EYES HAD AN AWESTRUCK EXPRESSION. HE GAWKED IN THE DIRECTION OF THE FIGHT.

HE CAME TO A FENCE AND CLAMBERED OVER IT. ON THE FAR SIDE, THE GROUND WAS LITTERED WITH CLOTHES AND GUNS. FOUR OR FIVE CORPSES KEPT MORNFUL COMPANY.

A HOT SUN HAD BLAZED UPON THE SPOT.

IN THIS PLACE THE YOUTH FELT THAT HE WAS AN INVADER. THIS FORGOTTEN PART OF THE BATTLE GROUND WAS OWNED BY THE DEAD MEN, AND HE HURRIED AWAY BEFORE ONE OF THE SWOLLEN FORMS WOULD TELL HIM TO BE BEGONE.

HE FINALLY CAME TO A LANE WHERE A BLOOD-STAINED CROWD STREAMED TOWARD THE REAR. THE WOUNDED MEN WERE CURSING, GROANING, AND WAILING

ONE WAS MARCHING WITH THE AIR IMITATIVE OF SOME SUBLIME DRUM MAJOR. UPON HIS FEATURES WAS AN UNHOLY MIXTURE OF MERRIMENT AND AGONY. AS HE MARCHED HE SANG A BIT OF DOGGEREL IN A HIGH AND QUAVERING VOICE:

SING A SONG AH VIC'TRY, A POCKET FULL AH BULLETS, FIVE AN' TWENTY DEAD MEN BAKED IN A PIE.

SOME ALREADY HAD THE GRAY SEAL OF DEATH UPON THEIR FACES: LIPS CURLED IN HARD LINES AT TEETH CLENCHED. OTHERS PROCEEDED SULLENLY, FULL OF ANGER AND THEIR WOUNDS, AND READY TO TURN UPON ANYTHING AS AN OBSCURE CAUSE.

THE YOUTH JOINED THIS CROWD AND MARCHED ALONG WITH IT. THE TORN BODIES EXPRESSED THE AWFUL MACHINERY IN WHICH THE MEN HAD BEEN ENTANGLED.

THERE WAS A TATTERED MAN, FOULED WITH DUST, BLOOD AND POWDER STAIN FROM HAIR TO SHOES, WHO TRUDGED QUIETLY AT THE YOUTH'S SIDE.

WAS PRETTY GOOD FIGHT, WA'N'T IT?

WHAT?

65

BUT THE TALL SOLDIER CONTINUED TO BE IN A LOWLY WAY. HE HUNG BABE LIKE TO THE YOUTH'S ARM. HIS EYES ROLLED IN THE WILDNESS OF HIS TERROR.

I WAS ALLUS A GOOD FRIEND T' YEH, WA'N'T I, HENRY? I'VE ALLUS BEEN A PRETTY GOOD FELLA?

THE TALL SOLDIER SUDDENLY SEEMED TO FORGET ALL HIS FEARS. HE BECAME AGAIN THE GRIM, STALKING SPECTER OF A SOLDIER. HE PUSHED THE YOUTH AWAY.

NO, NO, NO, LEAVE ME BE. LEAVE ME BE...

THE TALL SOLDIER WENT STAGGERING THROUGH THE GRASS BESIDE THE ROAD. THE YOUTH AND THE TATTERED MAN FOLLOWED CLOSELY.

LEAVE ME BE, LEAVE ME BE...

GAWD! HE'S RUNNIN'!

WHERE YEH GOIN', JIM? WHAT'S THE MATTER WITH YOU? TELL ME, WON'T YOU, JIM.

LEAVE ME BE, CAN'T YEH? LEAVE ME BE FER JUST A MINUTE.

THE YOUTH AND THE TATTERED MAN HUNG BACK BUT CONTINUED TO FOLLOW AS THE TALL SOLDIER STUMBLED ACROSS THE GRASSY FIELD

THE TALL SOLDIER STOPPED, AS IF HE HAD FOUND THE SPOT HE WAS LOOKING FOR... HE STOOD MOTIONLESS FOR A MOMENT. THEN HIS FORM STIFFENED AND STRAIGHTENED.

THERE WAS A SLIGHT RENDING SOUND. THEN HE BEGAN TO SWING FORWARD, FALLING LIKE A GIANT TREE.

THE YOUTH ROLLED TO HIS FRIEND AND ROLLED HIM OVER. HIS BLUE COAT FLAP FELL OPEN. HIS SIDE LOOKED AS IF IT HAD BEEN CHEWED BY WOLVES.

68

69

HE BECAME AWARE THAT THE FURNACE ROAR OF THE BATTLE WAS GROWING LOUDER. GREAT BROWN CLOUDS HAD FLOATED TO THE STILL HEIGHTS OF AIR BEFORE HIM. THE ROADWAY WAS NOW A CRYIING MASS OF WAGONS, TEAMS AND MEN...

THE YOUTH FELT COMFORTED IN A MEASURE BY THIS SIGHT. THEY WERE ALL RETREATING.

THEN HE SAW A FORWARD-GOING COLUMN OF INFANTRY ON THE ROAD. IT CAME SWIFTLY ON. THE YOUTH WONDERED WHAT THOSE MEN HAD EATEN THAT THEY COULD BE IN SUCH HASTE TO FORCE THEIR WAY TO GRIM CHANCES OF DEATH.

THE MEN AT THE HEAD BUTTED MULES WITH THEIR MUSKET STOCKS. THEY PRODDED TEAMSTERS INDIFFERENT TO ALL HOWLS.

THE COMMANDS TO MAKE WAY HAD THE RING OF GREAT IMPORTANCE IN THEM.

70

THE HASTE OF THE COLUMN TO REACH THE BATTLE SEEMED TO THE FORLORN YOUNG MAN TO BE SOMETHING MUCH FINER THAN STOUT FIGHTING. HEROES, HE THOUGHT, COULD FIND EXCUSES IN THE LONG SEETHING LANE.

FOR A FEW MOMENTS HE WANTED TO JOIN THEM IN THEIR FLYING TO THE FRONT. THEN THE DIFFICULTIES OF THE THING BEGAN TO DRAG AT HIM. HE HAD NO RIFLE.

THEY COULD RETIRE WITH PERFECT SELF-RESPECT AND MAKE EXCUSES TO THE STARS.

WELL, RIFLES COULD BE HAD FOR THE PICKING.

IN DESPAIR, HE DECLARED THAT HE WAS NOT LIKE THOSE OTHERS. HE NOW CONCEDED IT TO BE IMPOSSIBLE THAT HE SHOULD EVER BECOME A HERO. HE WAS A CRAVEN LOON. HE DENOUNCED HIMSELF AS A VILLAIN. HE SAID THAT HE WAS THE MOST UNUTTERABLY SELFISH MAN IN EXISTENCE.

HIS MIND PICTURED THE SOLDIERS WHO WOULD PLACE THEIR DEFIANT BODIES BEFORE THE SPEAR OF THE YELLING BATTLE FIEND, AND AS HE SAW THEIR DRIPPING CORPSES ON AN IMAGINED FIELD, HE SAID THAT HE WAS A MURDERER.

SUDDENLY WAVES OF MEN CAME SWEEPING OUT OF THE WOODS AND DOWN THROUGH THE FIELDS. HE KNEW AT ONCE THAT THE STEEL FIBERS HAD BEEN WASHED FROM THEIR HEARTS,

SAY, WHERE DE PLANK ROAD? WHERE DE PLANK ROAD.

THE YOUTH CLUTCHED A MAN B THE THE ARM. HE WAS HEAVING AND PANTING.

WHY, WHY, WHAT'S THE MATTER?

LET GO ME! LET GO ME!

WHY, WHY

WELL, THEN...

THE YOUTH'S FINGERS TURNED TO PASTE UPON THE OTHER'S ARM. HE SAW THE FLAMING WINGS OF LIGHTNINGFLASH BEFORE HIS VISION.

SUDDENLY, HIS LEGS SEEMED TO DIE.

HE FOUGHT AN INTENSE BATTLE WITH HIS BODY. HIS DULL SENSES WISHED HIM TO SWOON AND HE OPPOSED THEM STUBBORNLY.

ONCE HE PUT HIS HAND ON HIS HEAD AND TIMIDLY TOUCHED THE WOUND. THE SCRATCHING PAIN OF THE CONTACT MADE HIM DRAW A LONG BREATH THROUGH HIS CLINCHED TEETH.

HE HURRIED ON IN THE DUSK. THE DAY HAD FADED UNTIL HE COULD BARELY DISTINGUISH A PLACE FOR HIS FEET.

73

74

THE LOUD SOLDIER FINISHED HIS SENTRY DUTY, AND CLEANED AND BANDAGED THE YOUTH'S WOUND.

THERE. YEH LOOK LIKE THE DEVIL, BUT I BET YEH FEEL BETTER.

THERE, NOW, LIE DOWN AN' GET SOME SLEEP.

THE YOUTH, WITH HIS MANNER OF DOG LIKE OBEDIENCE, STRETCHED OUT WITH A MURMUR OF RELIEF AND COMFORT. THE GROUND FELT LIKE THE SOFTEST COUCH.

HE HAD PERFORMED HIS MISTAKES IN THE DARK, SO HE WAS STILL A MAN.

WHEN THE YOUTH AWOKE IT SEEMED TO HIM THAT HE HAD BEEN ASLEEP FOR A THOUSAND YEARS. GRAY MIST WERE SLOWLY SHIFTING BEFORE THE FIRST EFFORTS OF THE SUN'S RAYS.

WELL, HENRY, OL' MAN. HOW DO YOU FEEL THIS MORNING.

OH, LORD, I FEEL PRETY BAD.

77

THE YOUTH TOOK NOTE OF A REMARKABLE CHANGE IN HIS COMRADE SINCE THOSE DAYS OF CAMP LIFE UPON THE RIVER BANK.

HE SEEMED NO MORE TO BE CONTINUALLY REGARDING THE PROPORTIONS OF HIS PERSONAL PROWESS. HE WAS NO MORE A LOUD YOUNG SOLDIER.

WELL, HENRY, WHAT D'YEH THINK TH' CHANCES ARE? D'YEH THINK WE'LL WALLOP EM?

DAY B'FORE YESTERDAY, YOU WOULD A' BET YOU'D LICK THE HULL KIT-AN'-BOODLE ALL BY YOURSELF.

WELL, PERHAPS I WOULD.

I THOUGHT WE HANDLED EM PRETTY ROUGH YESTERDAY.

NOT A BIT! WHY, LORD, MAN, YOU DIDN'T SEE NOTHIN' OF THE FIGHT. WHY!...

THEN, A THOUGHT CAME TO HIM.

OH! JIM CONKLIN'S DEAD.

WHAT? IS HE? JIM CONKLIN?

YES. HE'S DEAD. SHOT IN THE SIDE.

YEH DON'T SAY SO. JIM CONKLIN... POOR CUSS!

78

79

THE YOUTH'S REGIMENT WAS MARCHED TO RELIEVE A COMMAND THAT HAD LAIN LONG IN SOME DAMP TRENCHES. THE MEN TOOK POSITIONS BEHIND A CURVING LINE OF RIFLE PITS THAT HAD BEEN TURNED UP, LIKE A LARGE FURROW, ALONG THE LINE OF THE WOODS.

B'JIMINEY, WE'RE GENERALED BY A LOT A LUNKHEADS!

MORE THAN ONE FELLER HAS SAID THAT T'-DAY.

IF WE FIGHT LIKE THE DEVIL AN' DON'T EVER WHIP, IT MUST BE THE GENERAL'S FAULT.

MEBBE YEH THINK YEH FIT TH' HULL BATTLE YESTIRDAY, FLEMING.

WHY, NO, I DON'T THINK I FOUGHT THE WHOLE BATTLE YESTERDAY.

OH!

80

THEY WERE MARCHED TO A CLEAR SPACE WHERE REGIMENTS AND BRIGADES, BROKEN AND DETACHED THROUGH THEIR ENCOUNTERS WITH THICKETS, GREW TOGETHER AGAIN AND LINES WERE FACED TOWARD THE PURSUING BARK OF THE ENEMY'S INFANTRY.

WHOOP-A-DADEE!

HERE WE ARE! EVERYBODY FIGHTIN'. BLOOD AN' DESTRUCTION!

GOOD GAWD! WE'RE ALWAYS BEING CHASED AROUND LIKE RATS! IT MAKES ME SICK! IT MAKES A MAN FEEL LIKE A KITTEN IN A BAG.

IT'LL ALL WORK OUT IN THE END.

OH, THE DEVIL IT WILL! YOU ALWAYS TALK LIKE DOG-HANGED PARSON...

YOU BOYS SHUT RIGHT UP! THERE'S NO NEED YOU WASTIN' YOUR BREATH IN LONG WINDED ARGUMENTS. ALL YOU GOT TO DO IS FIGHT, AN YOU'LL BE GETTIN' PLENTY IN ABOUT TEN MINUTES.

THERE'S TOO MUCH CHIN MUSIC AN' TOO LITTLE FIGHTIN' IN THIS WAR, ANYHOW.

THE DAY HAD GROWN MORE WHITE, UNTIL THE SUN SHED HIS FULL RADIANCE UPON THE THRONGED FOREST. A SORT OF GUST OF BATTLE CAME SWEEPING TOWARD THAT PART OF THE LINE WHERE LAY THE YOUTH'S REGIMENT.

A SINGLE RIFLE FLASHED IN A THICKET BEFORE THE REGIMENT. IN AN INSTANT IT WAS JOINED BY MANY OTHERS. THERE WAS A MIGHTY SONG OF CLASHES AND CRASHES THAT WENT SWEEPING THROUGH THE WOODS. THE BATTLE SETTLED TO A ROLLING THUNDER.

THERE WAS A PECULIAR KIND OF ATTITUDE IN THE MEN. THEY WERE WORN, EXHAUSTED, HAVING SLEPT BUT LITTLE AND LABORED MUCH, THEY ROLLED THEIR EYES TOWARD THE ADVANCING BATTLE AS THEY STOOD AWAITING THE SHOCK. THEY STOOD AS MEN TIED TO STAKES.

THE ADVANCE OF THE ENEMY HAD SEEMED TO THE YOUTH LIKE A RUTHLESS HUNTING. HE BEGAN TO FUME WITH RAGE AND EXASPERATION. YESTERDAY, WHEN HE HAD IMAGINED THE UNIVERSE TO BE AGAINST HIM, HE HAD HATED IT. TODAY HE HATED THE ARMY OF THE FOE WITH THE SAME GREAT HATRED.

IF THEY KEEP ON CHASING US. BY GAWD, THEY'D BETTER WATCH OUT.

CAN'T STAND TOO MUCH.

IF THEY KEEP ON A-CHASIN' US THEY'LL DRIVE US ALL INTEH TH' RIVER.

83

THE WIND OF BATTLE HAD SWEPT ALL ABOUT THE REGIMENT, UNTIL ONE RIFLE, INSTANTLY FOLLOWED BY OTHERS, FLASHED IN ITS FRONT.

A MOMENT LATER THE REGIMENT ROARED FORTH IN SUDDEN AND VALIANT RETORT.

THE BLUE SMOKE-SWALLOWED LINE CURLED AND WRITHED LIKE A SNAKE STEPPED UPON. IT SWUNG IT'S ENDS TO AND FRO IN THE AGONY OF FEAR AND RAGE.

THE FLAMES FIT HIM, AND THE HOT SMOKE BROILED HIS SKIN.

HIS RIFLE BARREL GREW SO HOT THAT ORDINARILY HE COULD NOT HAVE BORNE IT UPON HIS PALMS

BUT HE KEPT ON STUFFING CARTRIDGES INTO IT, AND POUNDING THEM WITH HIS CLANKING, BENDING RAMROD.

IF HE AIMED AT SOME CHARGING FORM THROUGH THE SMOKE, HE PULLED THE TRIGGER WITH A FIERCE GRUNT...

...AS IF HE WAS DEALING A BLOW OF THE FIST WITH ALL HIS STRENGTH.

ONCE HE, IN HIS INTENT HATE, WAS ALMOST ALONE, AND WAS FIRING, WHEN ALL THOSE NEAR HIM HAD CEASED. HE WAS SO ENGROSSED IN HIS OCCUPATION THAT HE WAS NOT AWARE OF THE LULL.

YEH INFERNAL FOOL, DON'T YEH KNOW ENOUGH T' QUIT WHEN THERE AIN'T ANYTHING T' SHOOT AT

GOOD GAWD.

THE LIEUTENANT WAS CROWING

BY HEAVENS, IF I HAD TEN THOUSAND WILD CATS LIKE YOU I COULD TEAR TH' STOMACH OUTA THIS WAR IN A WEEK.

ARE YEH ALL RIGHT, FLEMING? DO YEAH FEEL ALL RIGHT? THERE AIN'T NOTHIN' TH' MATTER WITH YEH, HENRY, IS THERE.

NO!

88

89

THERE WAS ONE SHOT THROUGH THE BODY, WHO RAISED A CRY OF BITTER AND PAINFUL LAMENTATIONS WHEN CAME THIS LULL. PERHAPS HE HAD BEEN CALLING OUT DURING THE FIGHTING ALSO, BUT AT THAT TIME NO ONE HAD HEARD HIM. BUT NOW THE MEN TURNED AT THE WOEFUL COMPLAINTS OF HIM UPON THE GROUND.

THE CHESTS OF THE MEN STRAINED FOR A BIT OF FRESHNESS, AND THEIR THROATS CRAVED WATER.

THE YOUTH'S FRIEND HAD A GEOGRAPHICAL ILLUSION CONCERNING A STREAM, AND HE OBTAINED PERMISSION TO GO FOR SOME WATER. IMMEDIATELY CANTEENS WERE SHOWERED UPON HIM.

THE YOUTH WENT WITH HIS FRIEND, FEELING A DESIRE TO THROW HIS HEATED BODY ONTO THE STREAM AND, SOAKING THERE, DRINK QUARTS.

NO WATER HERE.

THEY MADE A HURRIED SEARCH FOR THE SUPPOSED STREAM, BUT DID NOT FIND IT.

THEY TURNED WITHOUT DELAY AND BEGAN TO RETRACE THEIR STEPS. FROM THEIR POSITION AS THEY AGAIN FACED TOWARD THE PLACE OF FIGHTING, THEY COULD OF COURSE COMPREHEND A GREATER AMOUNT OF THE BATTLE THAN THEIR VISIONS HAD BLURRED BY THE HURLING SMOKE OF THE LINE.

THEY COULD SEE DARK STRETCHES WINDING ALONG THE LAND, AND ON ONE CLEARED SPACE THERE WAS A ROW OF GUNS MAKING GRAY CLOUDS, WHICH WERE FILLED WITH LARGE FLASHES OF ORANGE-COLORED FLAMES.

93

THE YOUTH STARED AT THE LAND IN FRONT OF HIM. ITS FOLIAGES NOW SEEMED TO VEIL POWERS AND HORRORS.

HE WAS UNAWARE OF THE MACHINERY OF ORDERS THAT STARTED THE CHARGE, ALTHOUGH FROM THE CORNERS OF HIS EYES HE SAW AN OFFICER COME GALLOPING, WAVING HIS HAT.

THE LINE FELL SLOWLY FORWARD LIKE A TOPPLING WALL, AND, WITH A CONVULSIVE GASP THAT WAS INTENDED FOR A CHEER, THE REGIMENT BEGAN ITS JOURNEY.

AS THE REGIMENT SWUNG FROM ITS POSITION OUT INTO A CLEARED SPACE THE WOODS AND THICKETS BEFORE IT AWAKENED. YELLOW FLAMES LEAPED FROM MANY DIRECTIONS. THE FOREST MADE A TREMENDOUS OBJECTION.

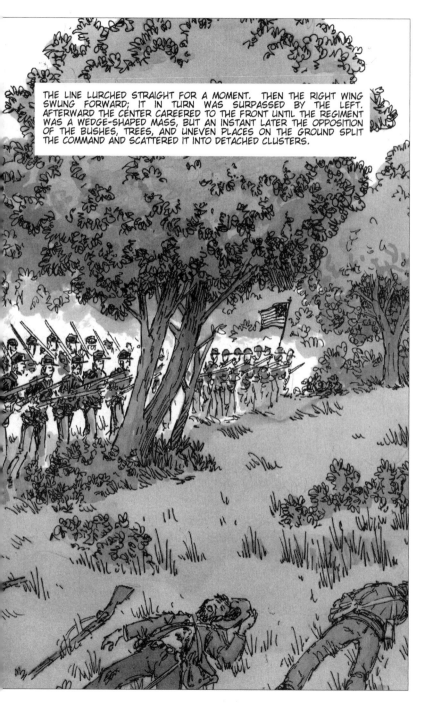

THE LINE LURCHED STRAIGHT FOR A MOMENT. THEN THE RIGHT WING SWUNG FORWARD; IT IN TURN WAS SURPASSED BY THE LEFT. AFTERWARD THE CENTER CAREERED TO THE FRONT UNTIL THE REGIMENT WAS A WEDGE-SHAPED MASS, BUT AN INSTANT LATER THE OPPOSITION OF THE BUSHES, TREES, AND UNEVEN PLACES ON THE GROUND SPLIT THE COMMAND AND SCATTERED IT INTO DETACHED CLUSTERS.

THE SONG OF THE BULLETS WAS IN THE AIR AND SHELLS SNARLED AMONG THE TREETOPS.

ZIP!

ZING!

MEN PUNCHED BY BULLETS FELL IN GROTESQUE AGONIES. THE REGIMENT LEFT A COHERENT TRAIL OF BODIES.

ONE SHELL TUMBLED DIRECTLY INTO THE MIDDLE OF A HURRYING GROUP AND EXPLODED IN CRIMSON FURY.

THE OPPOSING INFANTRY'S LINES WERE DEFINED BY THE GRAY WALLS AND FRINGES OF SMOKE.

KRAK!
KRAK!
KRACK!
KRAK!
KRAK!
KRAK!
KRACK!
KRAK!
KRAK!
KRACK!

THERE WAS A FRENZY MADE FROM THIS FURIOUS RUSH. THE MEN, PITCHING FORWARD INSANELY, HAD BURST INTO CHEERING, MOBLIKE AND BARBARIC, BUT TUNED IN STRANGE KEYS THAT CAN AROUSE THE DULLARD AND THE STOIC.

IT MADE A MAD ENTHUSIASM THAT, IT SEEMED, WOULD BE INCAPABLE OF CHECKING ITSELF BEFORE GRANITE AND BRASS.

100

PRESENTLY THE STRAINING PACE ATE UP THE ENERGIES OF THE MEN . AS IF BY AGREEMENT, THE LEADERS BEGAN TO SLACKEN SPEED.

SINCE MUCH OF THEIR STRENGTH AND THEIR BREATH HAD VANISHED, THEY RETURNED TO CAUTION. THEY WERE BECOMING MEN AGAIN.

THE YOUTH HAD A VAGUE BELIEF THAT HE HAD RUN MILES, AND HE THOUGHT IN A WAY, THAT HE WAS NOW IN SOME NEW AND UNKNOWN LAND.

THE MEN, HALTED, HAD OPPORTUNITY TO SEE SOME OF THEIR COMRADES DROPPING WITH MOANS AND SHRIEKS. A FEW LAY UNDER FOOT, STILL OR WAILING. AND NOW FOR AN INSTANT THE MEN STOOD, THEIR RIFLES SLACK IN THEIR HANDS, AND WATCHED THE REGIMENT DWINDLE.

THEY APPEARED DAZED AND STUPID.

THEN, ABOVE THE SOUND OF THE OUTSIDE COMMOTION, AROSE THE ROAR OF THE LIEUTENANT. HE STRODE SUDDENLY FORTH, HIS INFANTILE FEATURES BLACK WITH RAGE.

COME ON, YEH FOOLS!

COME ON! YOU CAN'T STAY HERE!

YOU MUST COME ON!

KRAK!

KA-POW!

POW!

HE STARTED RAPIDLY FORWARD, WITH HIS HEAD TURNED TOWARD THE MEN.

COME ON!

THE MEN STARED WITH BLANK AND YOKEL-LIKE EYES AT HIM. HE WAS OBLIGED TO HALT AND RETRACE HIS STEPS. HE STOOD THEN WITH HIS BACK TO THE ENEMY AND DELIVERED GIGANTIC CURSES INTO THE FACES OF THE MEN. HIS BODY VIBRATED FROM THE WEIGHT AND FORCE OF HIS IMPRECATION. AND HE COULD STRING OATHS WITH THE FAMILY OF A MAIDEN WHO STRINGS BEADS.

THE FRIEND OF THE YOUTH AROUSED. LURCHING SUDDENLY FORWARD AND DROPPING TO HIS KNEES, HE FIRED AN ANGRY SHOT AT THE PERSISTENT WOODS.

THIS ACTION AWAKENED THE MEN. THEY HUDDLED NO MORE LIKE SHEEP. THEY SEEMED SUDDENLY TO BETHINK THEM OF THEIR WEAPONS, AND AT ONCE COMMENCED FIRING.

BELABORED BY THEIR OFFICERS, THEY BEGAN TO MOVE FORWARD. THE REGIMENT, LIKE A CART INVOLVED IN MUD AND MUDDLE, STARTED UNEVENLY WITH MANY JOLTS AND JERKS. THE MEN STOPPED NOW EVERY FEW PACES TO FIRE AND LOAD, AND IN THIS MANNER MOVED SLOWLY ON FROM TREES TO TREES.

THE FLAMING OPPOSITION IN THEIR FRONT GREW WITH THEIR ADVANCE UNTIL IT SEEMED THAT ALL FORWARD WAYS WERE BARRED BY THE THIN LEAPING TONGUES, AND OFF TO THE RIGHT AN OMINOUS DEMONSTRATION COULD SOMETIMES BE DIMLY DISCERNED.

THE SMOKE LATELY GENERATED WAS IN CONFUSING CLOUDS THAT MADE IT DIFFICULT FOR THE REGIMENT TO PROCEED WITH INTELLIGENCE.

AS HE PASSED THROUGH EACH CURLING MASS THE YOUTH WONDERED WHAT WOULD CONFRONT HIM ON THE FARTHER SIDE.

THE COMMAND WENT PAINFULLY FORWARD UNTIL AN OPEN SPACE INTERPOSED BETWEEN THEM AND THE LURID LINES. HERE, CROUCHED AND COWERING BEHIND SOME TREES, THE MEN CLUNG WITH DESPERATION, AS IF THREATENED BY A WAVE.

THEY LOOKED WILD EYED, AND AS IF AMAZED AT THIS FURIOUS DISTURBANCE THEY HAD STIRRED. IN THE STORM THERE WAS AN IRONICAL EXPRESSION OF THEIR IMPORTANCE. THE FACES OF THE MEN, TOO, SHOWED A LACK OF A CERTAIN FEELING OF RESPONSIBILITY FOR BEING THERE.

108

CERTAINLY, JEST ACROSS TH' LOT! WE CAN'T STAY HERE.

COME ON!

THE PRIVATE FELT A SUDDEN UNSPEAKABLE INDIGNATION AGAINST HIS OFFICER.

COME ON YOURSELF, THEN!

THE FLAG, OBEDIENT TO THESE APPEALS, BENDED ITS GLITTERING FORM AND SWEPT TOWARD THEM.

THE MEN WAVERED IN INDECISION FOR A MOMENT, AND THEN WITH A LONG, WAILFUL CRY THE DILAPIDATED REGIMENT SURGED FORWARD AND BEGAN ITS NEW JOURNEY.

OVER THE FIELD WENT THE SCURRYING MASS. IT WAS A HANDFUL OF MEN SPLATTERED INTO THE FACES OF THE ENEMY. TOWARD IT INSTANTLY SPRANG THE YELLOW TONGUES. A VAST QUANTITY OF BLUE SMOKE HUNG BEFORE THEM. A MIGHTY BANGING MADE EARS VALUELESS.

THE YOUTH RAN LIKE A MAD MAN TO REACH THE WOODS BEFORE A BULLET COULD DISCOVER HIM. HE DUCKED HIS HEAD LOW, LIKE A FOOTBALL PLAYER.

WITHIN HIM, AS HE HURLED HIMSELF FORWARD, WAS BORN A LOVE, A DESPAIRING FONDNESS FOR THIS FLAG WHICH WAS NEAR HIM.

IT WAS A CREATION OF BEAUTY AND INVULNERABILITY. IT WAS A GODDESS, RADIANT, THAT BENDED ITS FORM WITH AN IMPERIOUS GESTURE TO HIM. IT WAS A WOMAN, RED AND WHITE, HATING AND LIVING, THAT CALLED HIM WITH THE VOICE OF HIS HOPES.

BECAUSE NO HARM COULD COME TO IT, HE ENDOWED IT WITH POWER. HE KEPT NEAR, AS IF IT COULD BE A SAVER OF LIVES, AND AN IMPLORING CRY WENT UP FROM HIS MIND.

IN THE MAD SCRAMBLE HE WAS AWARE THAT THE COLOR SERGEANT FLINCHED SUDDENLY, AS IF STRUCK BY A BLUDGEON. HE FALTERED, AND THEN BECAME MOTIONLESS, SAVE FOR HIS QUIVERING KNEES.

KRACK!

POW!

POW!

KRACK!

POK!

HE MADE A SPRING AND A CLUTCH AT THE POLE. AT THE SAME INSTANT HIS FRIEND GRABBED IT FROM THE OTHER SIDE.

THEY JERKED AT IT, STOUT AND FURIOUS, BUT THE COLOR SERGEANT WAS DEAD, AND THE CORPSE WOULD NOT RELINQUISH ITS TRUST.

FOR A MOMENT THERE WAS A GRIM ENCOUNTER.

THE DEAD MAN, SWINGING WITH BENDED BACK, SEEMED TO BE OBSTINATELY TUGGED, IN LUDICROUS AND AWFUL WAYS, FOR THE POSSESSION OF THE FLAG.

IT WAS PAST IN AN INSTANT OF TIME. THEY WRENCHED THE FLAG FURIOUSLY FROM THE DEAD MAN.

THE CORPSE SWAYED FORWARD WITH BOWED HEAD. ONE ARM SWUNG HIGH, AND THE CURVED HAND FELL WITH HEAVY PROTEST ON THE FRIEND'S UNHEEDING SHOULDER.

THE YOUTH AND HIS FRIEND HAD A SMALL SCUFFLE OVER THE FLAG.

GIVE IT T' ME!

NO! LET ME KEEP IT!

EACH FELT SATISFIED WITH THE OTHER'S POSSESSION OF IT, BUT HAD TO SHOW HIS WILLINGNESS TO FURTHER RISK.

THE YOUTH ROUGHLY PUSHED HIS FRIEND AWAY.

THE REGIMENT RESUMED ITS MARCH AGAIN, CURVING AMONG THE TREE TRUNKS. THE GREATER PART OF THE MEN, DISCOURAGED, THEIR SPIRITS WORN BY THE TURMOIL, ACTED AS IF STUNNED.

SHOOT INTO EM! SHOOT INTO EM, DAMN THEIR SOULS!

THE LIEUTENANT HAD BEEN SHOT IN THE ARM. IT HUNG STRAIGHT AND RIGID. OCCASIONALLY HE WOULD CEASE TO REMEMBER IT, AND BE ABOUT TO EMPHASIZE AN OATH WITH A SWEEPING GESTURE. THE MULTIPLIED PAIN CAUSED HIM TO SWEAR WITH INCREDIBLE POWER.

116

THE REGIMENT HAD RUN DOWN. THE MEN, HAVING HURLED THEMSELVES IN PROJECTILE FASHION, HAD PRESENTLY EXTENDED THEIR FORCES. THEY SLOWLY RETREATED, WITH THEIR FACES STILL TOWARD THE SPLUTTERING WOODS, AND THEIR HOT RIFLES STILL REPLYING TO THE DIN.

THE YOUTH HARANGUED HIS FELLOWS, PUSHING AGAINST THEIR CHEST WITH HIS FREE HAND. TO THOSE HE KNEW WELL HE MADE FRANTIC APPEALS, BESEECHING THEM BY NAME. HE WANTED REVENGE UPON THE OFFICER WHO HAD REFERRED TO HIM AND HIS FELLOWS AS MULE DRIVERS.

AND NOW THE RETREAT OF THE MULE DRIVERS WAS A MARCH OF SHAME TO HIM.

BUT THE REGIMENT WAS A MACHINE RUNDOWN. IT WAS DIFFICULT TO THINK OF REPUTATION WHEN OTHERS WERE THINKING OF SKINS, WOUNDED MEN WERE LEFT CRYING WHERE THEY LAY.

THE WAY SEEMED ETERNAL. IN THE CLOUDED HAZE MEN BECAME PANIC STRICKEN WITH THE THOUGHT THAT THEY MIGHT HAVE LOST THEIR PATH AND WERE PROCEEDING IN A PERILOUS DIRECTION.

THEY SUDDENLY REALIZED THAT THEY HAD BEEN FIRED UPON FROM POINTS WHICH THEY HAD CONSIDERED TO BE TOWARD THEIR OWN LINES.

118

THE OFFICERS LABORED LIKE POLITICIANS TO BEAT THE MASS INTO A PROPER CIRCLE TO FACE THE MENACES. THE MEN CURLED INTO DEPRESSIONS AND FITTED THEMSELVES SNUGLY BEHIND WHATEVER WOULD FRUSTRATE A BULLET.

THE YOUTH NOTED WITH VAGUE SURPRISE THAT THE LIEUTENANT WAS STANDING MUTELY. HE WONDERED WHAT HAD HAPPENED TO HIS VOCAL ORGANS THAT HE HAD NO MORE CURSES.

THERE WAS SOMETHING CURIOUS IN THIS LITTLE INTENT PAUSE. HE WAS LIKE A BABE WHICH, HAVING WEPT ITS FILL, RAISES ITS EYES AND FIXES THEM UPON A DISTANT TOY.

THEN HIS EYES WIDENED, AND HIS SOFT UNDER LIP QUIVERED FROM SELF-WHISPERED WORDS.

THE TWO BODIES OF TROOPS EXCHANGED BLOWS IN THE MANNER OF A PAIR OF BOXERS. THE FAST ANGRY FIRING WENT BACK AND FORTH....

THE MEN IN BLUE WERE INTENT WITH THE DESPAIR OF THEIR CIRCUMSTANCES AND THEY SEIZED UPON THE REVENGE TO BE HAD AT CLOSE RANGE. THE YOUTH HAD A SWEET THOUGHT THAT IF THE ENEMY WAS ABOUT TO SWALLOW THE REGIMENT, AT LEAST THEY HAD THE CONSOLATION OF GOING DOWN WITH BRISTLES FORWARD.

THE BLOWS OF THE ANTAGONIST BEGAN TO GROW MORE WEAK. WHEN THE MIST LIFTED, THEY SAW A GROUND VACANT OF FIGHTERS EXCEPT FOR THE CORPSES THAT LAY THROWN AND TWISTED INTO FANTASTIC SHAPES UPON THE SWARD.

THE MEN IN BLUE SPRANG OUT FROM BEHIND THEIR COVER, SOME OF THEM DANCING WITH JOY. THIS SMALL DUEL SHOWED THEM THAT THE PROPORTIONS WERE NOT IMPOSSIBLE. THE IMPETOUS OF ENTHUSIASM WAS THEIRS AGAIN. THEY GAZED ABOUT THEM WITH LOOKS OF UPLIFTED PRIDE, FEELING NEW TRUST IN THE GRIM, ALWAYS CONFIDENT WEAPONS IN THEIR HANDS.

AND THEY WERE MEN.

ALL WAYS SEEMED OPEN TO THEM. IN THE DISTANCE THERE WERE MANY COLOSSAL NOISES, BUT IN ALL THIS PART OF THE FIELD THERE WAS A SUDDEN STILLNESS....

IN THIS LAST LENGTH OF JOURNEY THE MEN BEGAN TO SHOW STRANGE EMOTIONS. THEY HURRIED WITH NERVOUS FEAR AND BACKWARD LOOKS OF PERTURBATION.

IT WAS PERHAPS THAT THEY DREADED TO BE KILLED IN INSIGNIFICANT WAYS AFTER THE TIMES FOR PROPER MILITARY DEATHS HAD PASSED.

AS THEY APPROACHED THEIR OWN LINES THERE WAS SOME SARCASM EXHIBITED ON THE PART OF A GAUNT AND BRONZED REGIMENT THAT LAY RESTING IN THE SHADE OF THE TREES.

WHERE TH' HELL YEH BEEN?

WHAT YEH COMIN' BACK FER?

WAS IT WARM OUT THEIR, BOYS?

THE YOUTH'S TENDER FLESH WAS DEEPLY STUNG BY THESE REMARKS.

THEY TURNED WHEN THEY ARRIVED AT THEIR POSITION TO REGARD THE GROUND OVER WHICH THEY HAD JUST CHARGED. THE YOUTH WAS SMITTEN WITH ASTONISHMENT.

THE DISTANCE NOW SEEMED TRIVIAL AND RIDICULOUS.

124

THE OFFICER WHO HAD FIRST REFERRED TO THEM AS MULE DRIVERS CAME GALLOPING UP TO THEIR REGIMENT'S COMMANDER....

OH, THUNDER, MCCHESNAY, WHAT AN AWFUL BULL YOU MADE OF THINGS! YOU STOPPED ABOUT A HUNDRED FEET THIS SIDE OF A VERY PRETTY SUCCESS!

WHAT A BUNCH OF MUD DIGGERS YOU'VE GOT ANYWAY.

OH, WELL GENERAL, WE WENT AS FAR AS WE COULD.

HEARING THIS, THE YOUNG LIEUTENANT WAS IN AN IMPOTENT RAGE!

I DON'T CARE WHAT A MAN IS, A GENERAL OR WHAT, IF HE SAYS TH' BOYS DIDN'T PUT UP A GOOD FIGHT OUT THERE HE'S A DAMNED FOOL!

LIEUTENANT, THIS IS MY OWN AFFAIR, AND I'LL TROUBLE YOU...

ALL RIGHT, COLONEL. ALL RIGHT.

THE NEWS THAT THE REGIMENT HAD BEEN REPROACHED WENT ALONG THE LINE, AND THE MEN WERE BEWILDERED AND ANGRY.

GOOD THUNDER!

HE MUST THINK WE WENT OUT THERE AN' PLAYED MARBLES!

125

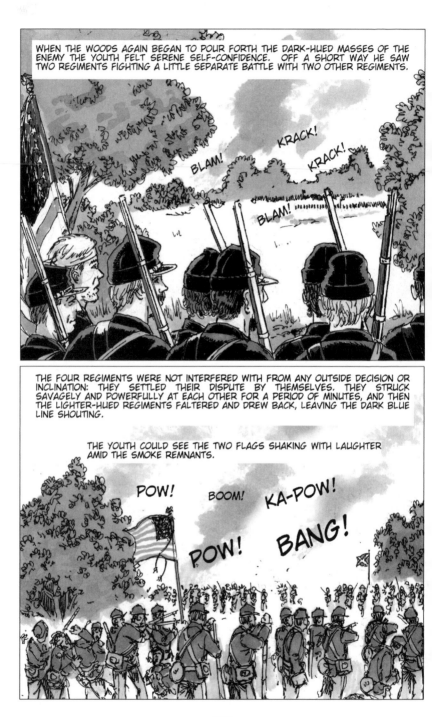

WHEN THE WOODS AGAIN BEGAN TO POUR FORTH THE DARK-HUED MASSES OF THE ENEMY THE YOUTH FELT SERENE SELF-CONFIDENCE. OFF A SHORT WAY HE SAW TWO REGIMENTS FIGHTING A LITTLE SEPARATE BATTLE WITH TWO OTHER REGIMENTS.

BLAM!

KRACK!

KRACK!

BLAM!

THE FOUR REGIMENTS WERE NOT INTERFERED WITH FROM ANY OUTSIDE DECISION OR INCLINATION: THEY SETTLED THEIR DISPUTE BY THEMSELVES. THEY STRUCK SAVAGELY AND POWERFULLY AT EACH OTHER FOR A PERIOD OF MINUTES, AND THEN THE LIGHTER-HUED REGIMENTS FALTERED AND DREW BACK, LEAVING THE DARK BLUE LINE SHOUTING.

THE YOUTH COULD SEE THE TWO FLAGS SHAKING WITH LAUGHTER AMID THE SMOKE REMNANTS.

POW!

BOOM!

KA-POW!

POW!

BANG!

SUDDENLY THE GUNS ON THE SLOPE ROARED OUT A MESSAGE OF WARNING. THE EMACIATED REGIMENT BUSTED FORTH WITH UNDIMINISHED FIERCENESS WHEN THE TIME CAME. WHEN ASSAULTED AGAIN BY BULLETS, THE MEN BURST OUT IN A BARBARIC CRY OF RAGE AND PAIN. THEY BENT THEIR HEADS IN AIMS OF INTENT HATRED BEHIND THE PROJECTED HAMMERS OF THEIR GUNS. THEIR RAMRODS CLANGED LOUD WITH FURY.

THE LIEUTENANT, AFTER HAVING HIS ARM BANDAGED, LET OUT STRINGS OF EXPLETIVES WHICH HE SWUNG LASHLIKE OVER THE BACKS OF HIS MEN.

THE YOUTH, STILL BEARER OF THE COLORS, DID NOT FEEL IDLENESS. HE WAS DEEPLY ABSORBED AS A SPECTATOR.

A FORMIDABLE LINE OF THE ENEMY CAME WITHIN DANGEROUS RANGE.

HE COULD BE SEEN PLAINLY — TALL, GAUNT MEN WITH EXCITED FACES RUNNING WITH LONG STRIDES TOWARD A WANDERING FENCE.

THE INSTANT THE MEN OF THE REGIMENT RECOGNIZED THE MENACE, THEY THREW UP THEIR RIFLES AND FIRED A PLUMPING VOLLEY AT THE FOE. THERE HAD BEEN NO ORDER GIVEN.

KRACK!
KRACK!
KRACK!
KRAK!
KRAK!
KRACK!
KRACK!

BUT THE ENEMY WAS QUICK TO GAIN THE PROTECTION OF THE LINE OF FENCE. THEY SLID DOWN BEHIND IT WITH REMARKABLE CELERITY, AND FROM THIS POSITION THEY BEGAN BRISKLY TO SLICE UP THE BLUE MEN.

THE BLUE REGIMENT BRACED THEIR ENERGIES FOR A GREAT STRUGGLE. THE YOUTH RESOLVED NOT TO BUDGE WHATEVER HAPPENED. IT WAS CLEAR TO HIM THAT HIS FINAL AND ABSOLUTE REVENGE WAS TO BE ACHIEVED BY HIS DEAD BODY LYING, TORN AND GLITTERING, UPON THE FIELD.

THE REGIMENT BLED EXTRAVAGANTLY.

THE FIRE OF THE REGIMENT HAD BEGUN TO WANE AND DRIP. THE ROBUST VOICE, WHICH HAD COME STRANGELY FROM THE THIN RANKS, WAS GROWING RAPIDLY WEAK.

KRAK!

KRACK!

KRACK!

EVEN THE LIEUTENANT, WHO CONTINUED TO CURSE, SEEMED TO BE USING UP HIS LAST BOX OF OATHS,

KA-POW!

BLAM!

BANG!

THE COLONEL CAME RUNNING ALONG THE BACK OF THE LINE:

WE MUST CHARGE'M!

WE MUST CHARGE'M!

IT WOULD BE DEATH TO STAY IN THE PRESENT PLACE, AND TO GO BACKWARDS WOULD EXALT TOO MANY OTHERS. HE EXPECTED THAT HIS COMPANIONS, WEARY AND STIFFENED, WOULD HAVE TO BE DRIVEN TO THE ASSAULT. BUT THERE WAS A NEW AND UNEXPECTED FORCE IN THE MOVEMENT OF THE REGIMENT. THEY WERE IN A STATE OF FRENZY.

IT APPEARED THAT THE SWIFT WINGS OF THEIR DESIRES WOULD HAVE SHATTERED THE IRON GATES OF THE IMPOSSIBLE.

THE YOUTH KEPT THE BRIGHT COLORS TO THE FRONT...

...AND CENTERED THE GAZE OF HIS SOUL UPON THE OTHER FLAG.

AS HE RAN A THOUGHT OF THE SHOCK OF CONTACT GLEAMED IN HIS MIND. HE EXPECTED A GREAT CONCUSSION WHEN THE TWO BODIES OF TROOPS CRASHED TOGETHER. IT SEEMED THAT IN TRUTH THERE WOULD BE A CLOSE AND FRIGHTFUL SCUFFLE.

THE MEN IN BLUE SHOWED THEIR TEETH.

BUT PRESENTLY HE COULD SEE THAT MANY OF THE MEN IN GRAY DID NOT INTEND TO ABIDE THE BLOW.

THE SWIRLING BODY OF BLUE MEN CAME TO A SUDDEN HALT AT CLOSE AND DISASTROUS RANGE AND ROARED A SWIFT VOLLEY.

KRAK!
KRACK!
KRACK!
KRACK! KRACK!
KRAK!
KRACK! KRACK!
KRAK!
KRACK!
KRAK!
KRAK!
KRAK!

THE GROUP IN GRAY WAS SPLIT AND BROKEN BY THIS FIRE, BUT ITS RIDDLED BODY STILL FOUGHT.

TOTTERING AMONG THEM WAS THE RIVAL COLOR BEARER WITH THE BLEACH OF DEATH OVERTAKING HIS FACE.

THE MEN IN BLUE YELLED AGAIN AND RUSHED IN UPON THEM. THE YOUTH'S FRIEND WENT OVER THE OBSTRUCTION IN A TUMBLING HEAP.

HE SPRANG AT THE FLAG AS A PANTHER AT PREY. HE PULLED AT IT AND, WRENCHING IT FREE, SWUNG UP ITS RED BRILLIANCY WITH A MAD CRY OF EXULTATION.

THE COLOR BEARER, GASPING, LURCHED OVER IN A FINAL THROE AND, STIFFENING CONVULSIVELY, TURNED HIS HEAD FACE TO THE GROUND.

THERE WAS MUCH BLOOD UPON THE GRASS.

AT ONE PART OF THE LINE FOUR MEN HAD BEEN SWOOPED UPON, AND THEY NOW SAT AS PRISONERS. ONE WAS NURSING A WOUND IN THE FOOT. HE CUDDLED IT, BABY-WISE, BUT HE LOOKED UP FROM IT OFTEN TO CURSE WITH AN ASTONISHING UTTER ABANDON AT THE NOSES OF HIS CAPTORS.

ANOTHER, WHO WAS A BOY IN YEARS, TOOK HIS PLIGHT WITH GREAT CALMNESS AND APPARENT GOOD NATURE. HE CONVERSED WITH THE MEN IN BLUE, STUDYING THEIR FACES WITH BRIGHT AND KEEN EYES.

THE THIRD CAPTIVE PRESERVED A STOICAL AND COLD ATTITUDE. TO ALL ADVANCES HE MADE ONE REPLY WITHOUT VARIATION, "AH, GO T' HELL!"

THE LAST OF THE FOUR WAS ALWAYS SILENT AND, FOR THE MOST PART, KEPT HIS FACE TURNED IN UNMOLESTED DIRECTIONS. IT LOOKED LIKE SHAME WAS UPON HIM, AND WITH IT PROFOUND REGRET THAT HE WAS, PERHAPS, NO MORE TO BE COUNTED IN THE RANKS OF HIS FELLOWS.

THERE WAS SOME LONG GRASS. THE YOUTH NESTLED IN IT AND RESTED, MAKING A CONVENIENT RAIL TO SUPPORT THE FLAG.

HE BEGAN TO STUDY HIS DEEDS, HIS FAILURES AND ACHIEVEMENTS.

THE GHOST OF HIS FLIGHT FROM THE FIRST ENGAGEMENT APPEARED TO HIM AND DANCED.

THE REGIMENT MARCHED UNTIL IT JOINED ITS FELLOW REGIMENTS, RE-FORMING THE BRIGADE.

IT RAINED. THE PROCESSION OF WEARY SOLDIERS BECAME A BEDRAGGLED TRAIN, DESPONDENT AND MUTTERING, MARCHING WITH CHURNING EFFORT IN A TROUGH OF LIQUID BROWN.

SO IT CAME TO PASS THAT AS HE TRUDGED FROM THE PLACE OF BLOOD AND WRATH HIS SOUL CHANGED. SCARS FADED AS FLOWERS. HE HAD BEEN TO SEE THE GREAT DEATH, AND FOUND THAT, AFTER ALL IT WAS BUT THE GREAT DEATH.

HE WAS A MAN.

146

THE YOUTH SMILED, FOR HE SAW THAT THE WORLD WAS A WORLD FOR HIM...

...THOUGH MANY DISCOVERED IT TO BE MADE OF OATHS AND WALKING STICKS.

HE HAD RID HIMSELF OF THE RED SICKNESS OF BATTLE. THE SULTRY NIGHTMARE WAS IN THE PAST.

HE HAD BEEN AN ANIMAL BLISTERING AND SWEATING IN THE HEAT AND PAIN OF WAR.

HE TURNED NOW WITH A LOVER'S THIRST TO IMAGES OF TRANQUIL SKIES, FRESH MEADOWS, COOL BROOKS...AN EXISTENCE OF SOFT AND ETERNAL PEACE.